FIFTH-GRADE
SECRETS

BY JANET ADELE BLOSS

cover art by Gabriel
inside illustration by Mel Crawford

Published by Willowisp Press
801 94th Avenue North, St. Petersburg, Florida 33702

This edition copyright © 1994 by Willowisp Press,
a division of PAGES, Inc.
Original edition © 1985 by Willowisp Press

Printed in the United States of America

2 4 6 8 10 9 7 5 3 1

ISBN 0-87406-695-6

December 8, 1839

. . . I woke this morn with devout thanksgiving
for my friends, the old and the new. I think
no man in the planet has a circle more
noble. They have come to me unsought: the
great God gave them to me.

Ralph Waldo Emerson

One

I didn't complain about the sleeping bags, the water diet, the oatmeal facials, or the wool underwear. But when I got home from summer camp and found the refrigerator full of alfalfa sprouts, yogurt, bok choy, and tofu, I just had to say something.

"What's all this garbage?" I yelled.

"Why, Billie Casey!" my mother said. "You don't need to yell."

"Yuck!" I shouted. "Mom, where's the real food? Where are the chocolate bars, cookies, malted milk balls, and stuff?" I opened every cabinet in the kitchen looking for them, but all I could find was new weird-looking stuff in jars and boxes.

Mom came into the kitchen and smiled like nothing was wrong. "Now, honey," she said, "it's health food. We've been eating too much red meat and candy. It's bad for you. I've decided that we're going to eat more sensibly from now on. So while you were away at camp I threw out all of the foods with sugar in them."

I pinched myself to make sure I wasn't having a nightmare. This was beginning to look pretty bad.

"Do chocolate bars count as sugar?" I asked.

"You bet they do!" Mom said. "Chocolate bars are the worst of all. Those were the very first things that I threw out."

"No more Snickers?" I asked.

Mom shook her head. "No more Snickers," she said.

That was the last straw. If there's one thing an eleven-year-old girl needs lots of, it's Snickers. I said, "Come on, Mom. Give me a break. Isn't there anything decent to eat around here?"

Mom didn't hear me because she was

sitting on the kitchen floor doing yoga exercises. Yoga is when you sit all bent up like a pretzel, close your eyes and hum, all at the same time. It looks kind of weird, but then I guess my mom's kind of weird. She says that doing yoga exercises makes her feel good. It's funny, because she always seems a lot happier after she does them. Maybe it works.

My mom's the type of person who likes to try new things even if they look strange. Like one summer she wore flowers in her hair for a whole week. She said it made her feel like a wild girl of the forest. See what I mean? My mom's weird.

I don't mind it so much when she gets into her fads by herself, but sometimes she drags me into them, too. One time she had the idea that we should sleep in sleeping bags on the living room floor at night. That was right after the divorce. Dad had just moved out and into an apartment in Columbia City, and I think Mom was feeling kind of lonely. Maybe she needed an excuse to sleep with me on the living room floor so she'd have someone to talk to.

Sleeping in a sleeping bag wasn't too bad, either. Mom and I stayed up late talking and laughing. I was just getting used to it when Mom started putting sofa cushions under her sleeping bag. Then by the end of the week she was saying stuff like, "Billie, are you tired of this, honey? We can stop whenever you want to."

I knew it wouldn't be much longer before she got tired of it and sure enough, when I got home from school on Friday, the sleeping bags had disappeared. That's just how my mom is. She likes to try new things. She'll read about something weird in a magazine and then she'll try it. Then she gets tired of it. I guess you could say she's into fads. So, when I got home from summer camp and found out that she'd thrown out all the candy and good stuff, I guess I shouldn't have been surprised. But I was.

While Mom was doing her yoga exercises, I went out to the backyard to say "hi" to my dog, Bonehead. He was lying in the backyard chewing on a bone as usual. That's how he got his name.

He jumped up when he saw me and wagged his tall like crazy. He ran over and jumped up on me. He's a pretty big dog and he always gets a footprint on each of my shoulders. I kind of like the smell of the mud he leaves.

Dad gave me Bonehead for my ninth birthday. He came in a white box with a big red bow. There were holes punched in the lid, so I knew right away there was a puppy in there. Also, I'd been leaving pictures of dogs all around the house as a hint. I was afraid if I didn't do something I might get a goldfish.

I remember when I opened the lid of the box. Bonehead burst out like a firecracker. He knocked me in the chin with his head. Then he slobbered on my ear, jumped on my mom and ripped her hose, chewed up my dad's work gloves, and scratched the paint off the kitchen door. What a great dog! I loved him from the first minute that I saw him!

When I got home from camp I played in the

backyard with Bonehead until I heard pots and pans rattling in the kitchen. Then I went back inside. Mom was getting dinner ready. She had a smile on her face like she always does after her yoga exercises.

"Where's the meat?" I asked, sniffing the air. There were strange smells in the air, but no meat smells.

"Billie, dear," Mother said. "Please don't upset my alpha waves."

Alpha waves are what Mom gets after she's done her yoga. I'm not sure what they are. But I think they're invisible waves that get hurt if you yell at them. Don't ask me. I'm just eleven. Maybe I'll get some alpha waves when I'm twelve I wouldn't mind having some if they made me want to smile all the time.

I wonder if there's a kind of wave that makes you want to cry all the time. I think there is. At least that's how I felt when I saw what we were having for dinner. I sat at the table and Mom handed me a bowl. It looked like it was full of seaweed.

"What am I, a fish?" I asked.

"Now, Billie," said my mother, "it's kelp. Just try it. It's good for you. It helps your eyesight."

There's nothing wrong with my eyesight, but I put some on my plate anyway. I hate to say it, but it looked kind of like snot. I scooped some onto my fork and then I tasted it. Talk about gross! I swallowed it in a big lump because it all stuck together in a blob.

"Have some tofu," Mom said. "It's good for your bones and teeth." She passed me another bowl. This stuff didn't look too bad. It was kind of like scrambled eggs, but more frizzled.

"What's tofu?" I asked.

"It's made from soy beans," Mom said. "It's high in protein. I read in a magazine that a famous model lost 35 pounds by eating it."

"I could lose 82 pounds easy," I said. I weigh 82 pounds.

I wonder why it is that whenever your parents start telling you that you should eat something because it's good for you, you can bet it's going to taste like rotten cheese. At least, that's what the tofu tasted like. I held my nose while I ate it. One thing I can say for it is that it wasn't as bad as the kelp. Then I remembered that if you put enough salt on something you can disguise the taste.

"Pass the salt, please," I said.

"Are you serious?" Mom asked. Her pink dangly earrings shook. "Do you have any idea what salt does to your arteries?" she asked.

"What are arteries?" I asked, eyeballing the table. I didn't see any salt.

"Why, Belinda Joan Casey! Arteries carry blood from your heart through your whole body! They get hard if you eat too much salt. You don't want them to get hard, do you?"

"I guess not," I said. Suddenly, I didn't feel hungry anymore. I think it was all that talk about bones, blood, protein, and soy beans.

"Don't worry, Billie, honey," Mom said. "You'll get used to the health food diet. Pretty

soon you'll feel so great you won't even want to look at another chocolate bar."

Oh, no. Why did Mom have to remind me of chocolate? That made me think of Snickers with chocolate, lots of nuts, and caramel. Ah-h-h-h, Snickers!

"After a few months, you'll be the healthiest girl in the whole state of Ohio," Mom said.

Yeah, I thought to myself. I'll also be the skinniest.

I went out to the backyard to see Bonehead again. He was still chewing on that old bone and I have to admit, it was beginning to look pretty good. It was either from a pork roast or a ham. I wasn't sure, so I walked over for a closer look.

No doubt about it. Mom's new food fad was going to drive me crazy. Hopefully she would be over it by the time school started. That was just two weeks away.

Two

"WHAT do you have, Kelly?" Amy asked. "I have ham and cheese with mustard. Yum!"

"I have roast beef on rye here," Kelly said. "Oh, good! Kosher dills, my favorite! What do you have, Billie?"

"A sandwich," I said. I wasn't taking any chances. I kind of slid the sandwich out of my bag so no one could see it. Ever since school started Mom was packing me weird lunches and it was embarrassing. My girl friends and I were sitting together at lunch just like we always did. Sometimes other people sat with us, too, but today it was just me, Kelly, and Amy.

I tried to hide my sandwich behind my napkin. Then I looked at it. Oh, no! Some hairy green stuff was hanging out the edges.

"Wow, look at that!" Amy said. "There's fungus on Billie's sandwich. What is it? Gross!"

Sometimes I feel like popping Amy in the snoot.

"It's just alfalfa sprouts," I said.

"Alfalfa?" Kelly said, laughing. "Isn't he the guy on *The Little Rascals*?" she asked.

Sometimes I feel like popping Kelly in the snoot, too.

"My mom's on a new kick," I explained. "She's on a health food diet. She only fixes crazy stuff for meals." That's what's great about Amy and Kelly. I can tell them about the weird things my mom does and they don't act shocked or anything. I didn't feel like punching them in the snoot anymore.

"What's that disgusting stuff?" asked Karla Branhurst. She walked up to the table and sat beside me. "Did you turn weird over the summer,

16

or what? What's that green stuff? Weeds?"
Karla opened her brown bag and I saw two
packages of chocolate cupcakes in there. I
could have just died.

Karla Branhurst is the sort of person that
can make you feel very embarrassed about
yourself. I mean, she's the sort of person who
would poke a camera under the door to take a
picture of you sitting on a toilet.

She's also the sort of person who would eat
four whole chocolate cupcakes by herself and
never offer to give you one single bite. I almost
died watching Karla eat those cupcakes. She
saved the chocolate icing on the top for last. Then
she ate it in little nibbles until it was all gone.

Boy! You should've seen the mouths chewing
around that table. I felt like I was in the middle
of a herd of cows—only they had the clover and
I had an old tennis shoe.

Kelly let a little chunk of roast beef fall from
her sandwich onto the floor and she just ignored
it. I couldn't believe it! I was dying to pick it up

and eat it, but of course I didn't. I was afraid I'd look like one of those people you see in the city who poke around in garbage cans.

I tried to hold my breath a lot so I couldn't smell the macaroni and cheese coming from the cafeteria. I munched into my sandwich. Strings of alfalfa sprouts hung out of my mouth. It's impossible to eat that stuff without pieces of it sticking out. It's kind of like eating spaghetti only it's a lot louder. Eating sprouts sounds like ten people eating popcorn at the same time.

I couldn't finish my gross sandwich, so I stuck it back in my bag. Then I pulled out my dessert. It was a brown granola square wrapped in wax paper. It looked like a dog biscuit. But I don't think even Bonehead would eat a granola square. There was a little folded note under the granola square. I unfolded it and read it. It said:

I love you, Billie!
Mom

"What's that?" asked Karla. She looked real interested. Her glasses flashed in my face.

"Nothing," I said. I slipped the note quickly into my pocket.

My mom surprises me sometimes. That little note gave me the courage to eat that granola bar. Boy, was it crummy. It was hard as a rock and tasted like sand mixed with glue. But I ate it anyway. I kept feeling my teeth with my tongue just to make sure they weren't breaking off. It's funny what a little love note will make you do.

The bell rang and it was time to go to my geography class. I really like geography. For my next birthday I want a globe because I think maps are too flat.

After school I met Amy and Kelly and we walked over to Amy's house. We shot some baskets because she has a basketball hoop in her driveway. None of us is very good at it, yet. But we keep practicing. I'd like to be the first girl in our school to try out for the boys' basketball team. Then I could play on the same team with Tim Kurtz. He's a guy in the sixth grade. He's real cute and he plays basketball and he's never even said one word to me. If I played on the basketball team with him he'd *have* to talk to me.

I've already made plans for what I'll do when I make the boys' basketball team. I'll be so good at it that I'll probably win medals and stuff. Tim and I will play basketball together after school. I'll shoot hook shots and I'll try to out jump him because he's taller than I am. He'll teach me how to guard, which is something I really need to work on. When I practice with Amy she screams every time I start waving my hands and hopping in front of her face.

After Tim and I play awhile he'll walk me home. He'll love Bonehead, and Mom will make us some cheeseburgers and french fries. It's a great daydream!

Amy and Kelly kind of pooped out and sat down in the grass by the driveway while I practiced shooting foul shots. Then, Amy's mother came out carrying a pitcher of lemonade and a plate of cookies. I almost fainted when I saw they were peanut butter squares with chocolate on top. Kelly ate two cookies and Amy ate three. I ate seven. I could've eaten seven more, but there weren't any left.

I guess I made a pig of myself. But it's the first good food I'd seen in two weeks, ever since my mom got into this stupid health food kick.

"Is your mother starving you?" asked Amy.

"No," I said. "I just don't like the food she makes anymore. It's not people-food. It's goatfood . . . weeds, flowers, and stuff like that."

"What are you going to do about it?" asked Kelly.

"Die," I said.

I really did feel like I was going to die if I had to eat any more tofu or sprouts. What if I turned into a vegetable? How would Mom like it if she came in to wake me up one morning and she found a giant carrot named Billie lying in my bed?

"Hey!" yelled Amy. "That's it! That's the answer!" Kelly and I looked at Amy like she was crazy.

"What are you talking about?" asked Kelly.

"Dying! That's it!" Amy said excitedly. "Pretend you're dying! Then your mother will *have* to start feeding you real food so you can live."

I thought about it for a minute. At first it seemed like a crazy idea, but it was the only one we had, so I said, "OK. I'll do it."

"Wow!" said Kelly. "How do you pretend to be dying?"

"I have some green eye makeup," said Amy. "My sister gave it to me. You could smear it all over your face . . . make it look like your skin's rotting off."

"OOO-oo-ooo gross!" cried Kelly.

"Good idea," I said. "Nice touch."

"Try to eat a raw egg," said Amy. "That'll make you throw up every time. Your mom will think you're dying if you throw up at least once a day."

"Won't she miss the eggs?" asked Kelly.

"Hmmm," sighed Amy. "I didn't think of that. I've got it! Mustard and milk. Mix it together. I learned about mustard and milk in Girl Scouts. It's guaranteed to make you barf your head off."

I wasn't so sure that I wanted to barf my head off. But I thought if it got Mom back to her old steak-grilling, pot-roasting self, I'd give it a try.

"I'd better be getting home," I said. "It's almost time for supper. Yuck."

"Are you coming to the park tomorrow?" asked Kelly. "Our Saturday roller-skating group is going to be there."

"No," I said. "I'm going to stay home tomorrow. I'll be pretty busy."

"What will you be doing" asked Kelly.

I grinned at my two friends.

"Dying," I said. "That's what I'll be doing tomorrow."

Three

"**B**ILLIE, honey! Aren't you out of bed, yet?" Mom poked her head in my bedroom door.

"I don't feel very well, Mom," I said. I spoke in a slow, scratchy old lady's voice. I even drooled on the pillow a little.

"I find that when I'm feeling a little under the weather, if I just pop out of bed, take a nice hot shower, and get into nice clean clothes, then I feel much, much better," said Mom. Then she closed the door and I heard her opening cabinets in the kitchen. That could mean only one thing. Mom was cooking up a mess of seaweed and mud for breakfast—or something just as gross.

I got out of bed and put on my robe. I figured that if I was really dying I wouldn't bother about shoes, underwear, and regular clothes. I wondered if dying people brush their teeth. Probably they do. So I did, too.

I have long black hair. When I don't comb it, it looks like I've been in a chicken fight. My dad used to tell me that I had hair like Black Beauty's tail. Black Beauty was a wonderful and beautiful race horse. My dad read the story to me when I was little, before he and Mom got divorced. But this morning my hair looked like Black Beauty's tail after a really long race. Good! That's just how I wanted it to look.

I only wore one slipper to show how bad my mysterious disease was. It made me walk lopsided which helped me look extra sick. I practiced limping around the room a few times before I went out to breakfast.

"*Guten morgen*, Billie darling," my mother

said. "I'm glad to see you're up. Don't you look lovely this morning!"

Guten morgen means good morning in German. My mother isn't even German so don't ask me why she says it.

I sat at my place at the table and Mom handed me a bowl. It was that same smelly tofu with the turmeric powder—in other words, fake scrambled eggs.

"Isn't there anything else to eat?" I growled.

"We have a special fast-energy strawberry smoothie to drink," Mom said. Her happy eyes widened like a fish's.

"What's that?" I asked suspiciously.

"It's like a milk shake," said Mom, "except it's for breakfast! Isn't that fun?"

I had to admit that it looked great with chunks of strawberries floating in it. But I knew there had to be a catch.

"How did you sweeten this?" I asked. "Sugar? I thought you weren't using sugar anymore."

"It's honey," Mom said. "Just the teensiest bit

of honey. Don't worry. It won't hurt your blood pressure."

"I'm not worried about my blood pressure," I said. "I'm only eleven. Eleven-year-olds don't have blood pressures. Pass the smoothie-fast, the fast-strawberry smoother, the strawber . . . oh, you know what I mean. Pass the milk shake, please."

"Gladly, dear," Mom said. She passed me the pitcher and I poured some of the smoothie into a glass. It looked thick and pink as it slid down the side of the glass.

I began to gulp it down. At first the coldness of it fooled me into thinking it tasted okay. But after a while the taste began to stick in my mouth.

"Mom," I asked, "what did you make this out of? Chalk?"

"Why, Belinda Joan Casey! What a rude thing to say!" Mom's lips kind of disappeared like they do when she's trying not to lose her temper.

"What is this stuff?" I asked.

"It's a fast-energy strawberry smoothie," she said.

"Come on, Mom. What's it made out of?" I demanded as I choked.

"Tofu. That's what's so wonderful about tofu. You can make *anything* with it," Mom said, smiling. Her lips were back. "It's easy! I just put a big chunk of tofu in the blender and it came out looking like cream."

"Tofu?" I yelled. "I thought you said this was a shake with honey in it!"

"Belinda Joan, don't raise your voice to me," Mom said. "I haven't done my yoga exercises and I don't have many alpha waves left as it is. I never said it actually was a milk shake and there *is* honey in it."

Mom took a sip of her smoothie. "Mmm-m-m, good," she said and licked her lips. But I don't think she really meant it. If you looked real close at the smoothie you could see gray streaks mixed in with the pink. It looked like the caulking Dad used when he stuck bathroom tiles back on the walls.

I have to admit it. Those chunks of strawberries had me fooled for a minute.

I suddenly remembered I was supposed to be dying. I pushed my plate away and put my head on the table.

"Billie, if you're tired, go back to bed, honey," Mom said.

I heard Mom start to clear the table and I opened one eye. I noticed she didn't finish her smoothie.

Okay. It was time for Plan Two—the green eye shadow. I walked back into my room and looked in the mirror. I put a touch of green under each eye. I smoothed it in so it wouldn't look too fake and I put some on my lips, too. I even put a little on my tongue. It tasted like tofu.

After I smoothed more green under my chin, I was ready. I walked into Mom's studio where she was painting. She always paints on Saturdays ever since she and Dad got divorced. She had a big canvas on a stand in front of her. She was dabbing paint on the canvas and squinting like she had an eyelash in her eye. I tried to think of cave men as I shuffled by Mom. I dragged my arms and breathed heavily.

"Stand over there, Billie." Mom pointed at the window. "Stand in the light and try not to slouch."

I shuffled over to the window. "What are you doing?" I asked.

"Painting you." Mom put a clean canvas on the stand. "Don't move."

I couldn't believe it. Here I was dying, and Mom wanted to paint me. Slowly I started to lay down on the floor by the window.

"Perfect!" said Mom. She turned her canvas sideways.

I moaned softly. Then I groaned loudly. I sounded like a cat with its tail being pulled.

"Billie, have you ever thought of taking singing lessons?" Mom asked. "I think you have a very fine voice."

Plan Two—the green eye shadow—wasn't working. Mom didn't even notice. I stuck my green tongue out, but she just kept talking about singing lessons. This seemed like a good time to begin Plan Three. I stood up and said, "I'll be right back, Mom. I have to go to the bathroom."

I shuffled slowly out of Mom's studio. Then I ran to the kitchen. I mixed up a big glass of mustard and milk. I swallowed the whole thing and waited for something to happen.

Just my luck, nothing did. In fact, it didn't taste bad at all. I wondered if eating all that tofu had ruined my taste buds. I mixed myself another glass of milk with tons of mustard in it this time. I drank it. Not bad. I licked my lips.

"Billie!" Mom called from the studio. "Hurry, dear! My paints are getting hard."

Plan Three didn't work. I felt fine. So it was time for Plan Four—shivering and shaking. I walked back to the studio, lay down by the window, and began to quiver like a big bowl of jello.

"Billie," said Mom, "what in the world are you doing?"

"I'm dying," I said. "I really am, Mom. No kidding. I'm dying from all this health food." I moaned, "OOO-oooooo."

Mom put her brush down and stared at me.

"But, honey," she started, "I'm doing it for your own good. All those chocolate bars you used to eat were bad for you. That stuff makes you sick."

"No, it doesn't, Mom," I said. I sat up on the floor to explain. "I ate seven cookies at Amy's house yesterday. They had chocolate, sugar, and peanut butter in them. I could've eaten fifty of them. They were great and I didn't feel bad at all."

Then suddenly I felt the worst ever. My ears felt hot and my stomach felt like someone was kicking it from the inside.

"Billie! What's wrong?" Mom cried. "You look sick!"

Amy forgot to tell me one thing about that

mustard and milk. It takes a little while for it to work, but when it finally does, watch out!

I moaned, "Ooo-oooooo." But this time it was for real. I ran for the bathroom, but I didn't make it.

Oops! Right in Mom's metal wastebasket. It was the one Dad got her at Disneyland. It has a picture of Minnie Mouse dancing in a red skirt on it. I could hear Mom behind me.

"It's those cookies," she said. "It's those horrible, horrible cookies with sugar and chocolate that you ate at Amy's!"

"No, it's not, Mom!" I tried to say. But it's not easy to talk when your head's in a wastebasket and your voice is echoing back at you.

"It's that darn chocolate," Mom said. "Well, we'll just have to be more careful about what we eat from now on, won't we? Maybe I should call Amy's mother and tell her not to give you any more cookies. It just makes you too sick!"

Oh, wow. Give me a break! I really felt like I was dying now. My face was sweating. My stomach hurt and I had my head stuck down in a smelly old metal can from Disneyland.

I had to think of a new plan, and fast!

Four

"COME on," I said. "I promise I won't ask again."

Amy shook her head. "Sorry, Billie," she said. "You've had dinner at our house twice already this week. I don't think my mom will let me ask you again. How about Kelly? Have you asked her?"

"Yeah," I said. "I asked her."

As a matter of fact, I'd had dinner at Kelly's once the week before, and twice the week before that. I even got her to switch lunches with me at school every Tuesday. On the other days I just threw my lunch away before I walked into the cafeteria. No one saw me do it and I was just too embarrassed to let people see the weird stuff Mom packed for me. Once she packed me a tofu McMuffin and a bottle of natural rhubarb juice. I got a kiwi for dessert. Boy, was that gross! So I began throwing my lunches away.

It wasn't as bad as I thought it would be because people started sharing their food with me. I think they felt sorry for me when I sat at the table and watched them eat. Once Esther Krillet gave me half of a real egg salad sandwich. And once Kelly gave me a package of orange Zingers.

One day Mary Jansen was just handing me a piece of cold fried chicken when Mrs. Butler walked up. She's my geography teacher.

"Where's your lunch, Billie?" she asked. "I notice you've been forgetting it lately."

"She doesn't bring her lunch," Karla said. "Since her parents got divorced, they don't have money for food anymore."

Remember Karla? I told you about her earlier. She's the kind of person you never want to go camping or roller-skating with. If she fell down and cut her knee she'd probably start screaming and check into a hospital.

"Is this true, Billie?" Mrs. Butler asked. "Doesn't your mother fix your lunch anymore?"

"No, ma'am," I said. "Not anymore."

I knew that was kind of a lie, but not a whole lie, because even though Mom was still fixing me food, I couldn't eat it. If I didn't eat it, then it wasn't really lunch. See? It might be lunch to my mom, but it wasn't lunch to me. It was goat food.

"Heavens!" exclaimed Mrs. Butler. "I knew this sort of thing went on in the cities, but I never expected it right here in Barnstown. Oh, you poor child."

Mrs. Butler leaned over and kissed the top of my head. She looked like she was going to cry for a minute. All the kids at the table began to giggle. I was glad when she finally walked away. But she came right back and stuck a sandwich under my nose.

"Eat this, you poor child," she said. "The least I can do is share my lunch with you."

The sandwich was kind of mashed, like maybe somebody sat on it on the bus. Also, it was a butter and grape jelly sandwich which is the one kind I can't stand. But I ate it anyway because Mrs. Butler stood right there until I finished it.

The bell rang and I was glad. But my next class was geography and Mrs. Butler walked the whole way with me since she teaches it.

She kept looking at me and saying, "You little lamb" and stuff like that. It was weird.

Mom got home late from work that night. She works in a topiary garden. That's where they use hedge clippers to cut bushes into the shapes of ducks and squirrels and things like that. We have a big bush by our kitchen door that's been cut into the shape of a dragon. It makes the neatest shadows in the moonlight. Whenever there was a full moon my dad used to say, "Look, Billie! There's a dragon on our back porch. I'll huff and I'll puff and I'll blow your house down!"

"That's the Three Little Pigs," I'd say, laughing. "And it was a wolf, not a dragon." I always loved nights with full moons.

"Honey, I'm home!" Mom called as she walked in the house. "What a day I've had! I did two squirrels, a panda bear, and an Indian on a pony. One of the Indian's legs is a little longer than the other one, but I can't be bothered with that. Whew! I think I need to sharpen the blade on my clippers." Mom kicked off her shoes and flopped into a chair. "How was your day, dear?" she asked.

"OK," I said. "Are you going to the PTA meeting tonight? Amy's mom said to tell you she needs a ride. Their car's in the shop."

"Oh, I completely forgot," said Mom, jumping out of her chair. "Can you get your own dinner, dear?" she asked. "I don't have time to do it if I'm going to make it to the PTA and pick up Ellen."

"Sure, Mom," I said. "I can make my own dinner."

I tried not to let my excitement leak out.

Whoopee! I'd go through every kitchen drawer and cabinet until I found something fit to eat. Tonight I'd have a real meal . . . no mung beans and no dried lily petals. Maybe I could even find some old forgotten bologna in the freezer.

Mom ran around and got ready. Then I heard her car pull out of the drive.

I ran to the kitchen and threw open the pantry door. I read the labels on all the boxes: millet, wheat berries, garbanzo beans, lentils. I had tasted them before and they all tasted like rocks, except for the millet. That was more like sand.

I reached back into a dark corner for a little plastic bag. It said "Chinese mushrooms—add water."

"OK," I said. "I will."

But when I added water the black thing in the bag began to unfold and grow bigger. It got to be the size of my hand when it stopped growing. I picked it out of the water, but it slipped from my fingers onto the floor. It looked like something I once saw in a movie called *Return of the King Blob.*

I poked a fork into it and carried it to the kitchen door. "Here, Bonehead!" I called, and threw the mushroom in the backyard. Bonehead came running over.

But even Bonehead wouldn't eat it. Instead he acted like it was a skunk. He shook his nose at it. Then he began to dig with his front paws and throw dirt on it. I guess dogs aren't so dumb.

I went back into the house and had a bowl of granola with milk. It wasn't too bad after I put pieces of banana on top of it. I was just too hungry to keep looking for meat and anyway, I knew that there probably wasn't any meat in the whole house.

I picked up a book I'd been reading and opened it. It was a book about a girl who was captain of a submarine that sailed under the ocean looking for the lost city of Atlantis. The girl found it, too. It was a beautiful city with rooftops made of pearl and stables full of friendly giant sea horses. The girl rode the sea horses around in the water. She had an oxygen tank so she could breathe.

I heard Mom's car in the driveway when I reached the part where the girl had to fight a giant octopus named Ivan the Awful.

"Belinda Joan Casey, come here right this minute," said Mom as she walked in the door. Just from her voice I could tell that her lips were disappearing. I'll bet if Ivan the Awful could talk, he'd sound just like Mom did right then.

"What is it, Mom?" I asked. "Did you lose your alpha waves?"

"Young lady, would you please tell me what all this business is about me starving you?" Mom asked. "I had three teachers come up to me tonight at the PTA and offer me money for food. Mrs. Butler said she gave you a sandwich today because I've quit making lunches for you. Would you please tell me what this is all about?"

I have to admit that my mom doesn't get mad very often. But when she does I usually wish I was on the moon, or in a submarine, or sleeping in the backyard with Bonehead, or anywhere but in the same room with my mom. I didn't know what to say. Mom kept talking.

"Mrs. Butler offered to take up a collection of money. I could've just died! And Mrs. Branhurst actually tried to give me a package of chicken weiners."

"Did you take them?" I asked hopefully.

"Belinda Joan Casey! It'll be a cold day in Hawaii when I accept chicken weiners from our neighbors!"

Mom looked me square in the eyes. "What have you been doing with your lunches?" she asked.

"Throwing them away," I said. There didn't seem to be much point in lying anymore. The lies were getting too tangled up and I didn't know what to say next.

"Throwing . . . ? You've been throwing . . . ?

All that good food?" Mom looked at me like I was the King Blob returning to Barnstown.

"I'm sorry," I said, and I meant it. "I won't do it again."

"Okay," said Mom. "I'll take your word for it. Let's not talk about it anymore. Case closed. I still love you."

That's another thing I like about my mom. She gets mad, but she doesn't stay mad. She took her jacket off and headed for the kitchen.

"Let's have a snack," said Mom.

"Okay," I said. I was glad to change the subject even if it meant eating something gross.

"How about some nice big Chinese mushrooms?" Mom asked. She smacked her lips. "Mmm-mm-mm. That would hit the spot."

Oh, no! Those Chinese mushrooms had already hit the spot, and that was a spot of dirt in the backyard. I admitted to using up all the mushrooms. Mom didn't say anything and she didn't get mad. She just sat on the floor like a pretzel, closed her eyes and began humming.

While her alpha waves were coming back I began thinking of a new plan to get some decent food. If this one didn't work, *nothing* would.

Five

I never threw my lunch away again after I promised my mom I wouldn't. The teachers at school quit trying to take up collections for me and Mom, and Mrs. Branhurst quit trying to give us her old chicken weiners. Since everyone saw me bringing my lunch they figured we weren't poor anymore. We never were really poor. That's just a story that Karla Branhurst spread around.

I brought my lunch every day. But I didn't sit in the cafeteria. It was just too embarrassing with everyone watching me eat fried tofu on bulgar bread with sprouts hanging out of my mouth. So I decided to find a place where I could eat alone.

Finally, I found the perfect place. It was

under the bleachers in the gym. I just walked right under there and sat in a dark corner way in the back. It was real dusty under there, but I figured at least no one could find me and laugh at my stupid lunches. It was kind of peaceful and quiet under there, too, for a change. It seems like when you're in school there's always about a million people around you. But under the bleachers it was nice. I was alone and I could think. That is, until one day when the worst thing that could happen to me happened.

I was sitting under the bleachers eating a bowl of wheat germ pudding. Suddenly the gym door flew open and there was all kinds of noise. All the sixth-grade boys came running out in their gym shorts and undershirts. They yelled and ran in circles. Some of them had basketballs that they dribbled and then shot into the hoop. Others did push-ups and jumping jacks.

I saw Tim Kurtz there. He was one of the best players. He hardly ever missed a shot, and he didn't shout and shriek like the others did.

After I watched the sixth-graders run around for a while, I figured out that it's the crummiest players who yell and scream the most. Maybe they think no one will notice that they never make a basket if they keep screaming. I don't know. It seems pretty silly to me.

I quit eating my wheat germ (another great lunch from Mom) and watched the boys play basketball. Mr. Cinder, the P.E. teacher, was there blowing his whistle and yelling at the guys.

I was glad I had on a navy blue sweater because it helped me fade into my dark corner. I pulled my knees in and sat all scrunched up, not moving a muscle. I felt pretty safe because the bleachers are big and I was hiding under them in the very back.

But all of a sudden it happened. My nose began to twitch and wiggle like a rabbit's. It felt like little firecrackers were exploding in my nose. That's always a sign that I'm going to sneeze. I thought if I blew the dust away maybe I wouldn't sneeze. So I took my lunch bag and fanned the dust away from me, but that just made it worse. Big clouds of dust swirled around me. It got in my eyes and nose.

Achoo! A-c-h-o-o! ACHOO! Whachooo! Oooaachooo!

I sneezed every kind of sneeze there was. When I finally stopped, I saw all the boys standing out on the basketball court. They were staring into the darkness under the bleachers. I sat real still and hoped they'd forget about me and go back to playing basketball. I even hoped there'd be a fire drill and they'd all run outside. But I had no such luck.

"Who's under there?" yelled Mr. Cinder. "Come out, right now!"

I was too scared to move. I couldn't stand the thought of all those boys laughing at me when I walked out with dust in my hair and cobwebs all over my jeans.

I just sat there like a rock. Then Mr. Cinder said, "Tim Kurtz, would you go under there and see what's going on?"

"Yes, sir," said Tim.

Great jumping tofu burgers! Tim Kurtz—the beautiful Tim, the one and only Tim, the Tim of my dreams, the best Tim in the world—was walking toward me! Boy, did I feel like a dumbhead. I was sure Tim would think I'm weird.

He looked around in the dark for a while. Then he must have seen me because he walked straight to me. He looked down at me through the bleacher seats and asked, "Aren't you Billie Casey?"

For a minute I thought I'd say, "No, sorry. You've made a mistake. My name is Karla Branhurst." But I knew he'd know I was lying, so I said, "Yup. I'm Billie."

"What are you doing under here?" Tim asked.

This was getting worse and worse. I couldn't even think of any good lies to tell. "Eating my lunch," I said.

"Why are you eating your lunch under the bleachers?" asked Tim.

I was so embarrassed. Here I was sitting

under the bleachers like an old dust mop. And who has to find me there? Tim Kurtz, the only boy in the whole school I liked. Tim Kurtz, the best player on the same basketball team that I wanted to be on. Tim Kurtz, with curly blond hair and a dimple in his chin. He looked at me waiting for an answer. I stood up and brushed off my jeans.

"It's a club," I said. "It's a secret club that no one knows about. We have to eat our lunch under the bleachers three times before we can join."

Tim just stared at me. I couldn't tell if he believed me or not.

"It's a great club," I said again, trying to smile.

Tim just kept staring. His blue eyes twinkled. One thing I've noticed is that when someone's eyes twinkle, that means they're nice. I like people whose eyes sparkle.

I stared back into Tim's sky blue eyes. He was so cute and I hardly ever got a chance to talk to him. But I couldn't think of anything to say so I began to walk by him.

"Wait, Billie!" called Tim. "There's something I want to ask you."

I couldn't believe it. Here I was leaving Tim Kurtz and he was calling me back to ask me something. I didn't know if Mom would let me go steady. Eleven years old might be too young for that. I stopped to let Tim catch up with me.

"Billie," he said, "can I join the club? Who's in it? What's the name of it?"

Oh, no! I had to think fast.

"It's kind of a secret," I said. "I don't really know that much about it."

"Don't you know the name of it?" asked Tim. "If I was in a club, I'd want to know the name of it."

"Tim Kurtz! What in the heck are you doing?" yelled Mr. Cinder. "Who are you talking to? Is someone else under there?" At this point I felt like shriveling up and dying.

Tim started to walk me to the gym door. Then all the sixth-grade boys began giggling and looking at us. Sometimes I can't believe how immature boys are. Mr. Cinder looked down at me. His belly hung over the top of his sweat pants. "Don't you have somewhere you're supposed to be, young lady?" he asked.

"Yes, sir," I said. I left the gym and went to the bathroom to wait until my next class started.

After lunch comes geography and Tim is in my class. When he walked by my desk he said, "Really, Billie. I want to know more about this club. It sounds fun. I'll be at your locker after school and you can clue me in."

Oh, brother! It was hard to listen to Mrs. Butler after that. All I could think about was what new lie could I tell Tim about the club. Maybe I could tell Tim that we had to forget the club because too many people wanted to join and it was getting to be too big.

After class Karla Branhurst came rushing up to me. She said, "Hey, Billie. I hear you're starting a new club. Can I be in it?"

"I don't know what you're talking about," I said.

"Everyone knows about it," said Karla.

"Tim Kurtz told Brad Efaw. Brad told me and I've been telling *everyone*. Is it true you asked all the sixth-grade boys to be in it?"

I tried to hurry away from Karla, but the hall was too crowded to get very far.

"Billie!" called Matt Roush from the water fountain. "I'll be at your locker after school. I want to be in the club, too."

Kelly walked by me, saying, "Thanks a lot for telling me about the club, Billie, old pal."

My next class was math and I didn't hear one word that Mr. Branden said. All I could think about was the mess I was in and how everyone was going to be waiting for me by my locker after school. I wondered if I should pretend to faint. I could fall on the floor with my eyes closed. Then everyone would feel sorry for me and call my mom to come and get me. But then I'd have to come to school the next day and face all the kids. I couldn't escape.

I wondered if I could get Mom to move to another state. Probably not. Another planet?

No way. Maybe I could change my name and dye my hair red. But all the kids would still recognize me. That wouldn't work either.

When I got to my next class, I found a note on my desk. It said:

Billie,
Please sign us up to be in your club. See
you after school!
                    Terry Kensler
                    Carol Ann Collins
                    Tom Carpenter
                    Tina Grouse
                    Beth Grant
                    Jill McGee
                    Mary Louise Land
                    Zippy Fernando
                    Bill White

I almost died when I read that note. What could I do? This was my last class and it was torture. I spent the whole hour watching the clock and worrying. I wondered how angry everyone would get at me when they found out there wasn't really a club. Would they all decide never to talk to me again? Would they tell the principal? Would no one ever sit by me on the bus again? Would Tim Kurtz think I was the grossest, ugliest, dumbest girl in the world?

Would Amy and Kelly not want to be friends with me anymore?

The bell rang. I ran to the bathroom and waited, trying to think of something to tell them. But I couldn't. So finally I came out and headed toward my locker. I almost turned and ran when I saw the crowd of people waiting for me there. It looked like the whole school was there.

"Here she comes!" someone yelled. Then they all started talking at once.

"Can I join?"

"What kind of club is it?"

"How many people are in it?"

"Are you the president, Billie?"

"Does it cost anything to join?"

"Who's in the club?"

"What's the name of it?"

Tim Kurtz was there, too. He smiled at me and waited for me to say something.

"Come on, Billie," said Karla Branhurst. "What's the big secret? What's the name of the club?"

"It's no secret," I said. I felt the lockers against my back. I could see my face reflected in Eddie Sinnot's glasses. I wasn't smiling and one of my eyebrows was jumping. My face looked like the face of a ghost I once saw in an old movie. As soon as I thought of that movie my mouth opened and words just kind of jumped out. I couldn't believe what I was saying. "It's the GHOST Club," I said. "Yup, that's it. It's the GHOST Club. Good club, too. Well, I gotta be going now. See you guys around."

"What the heck is the GHOST Club?" asked Karla. "I think you're just making this up."

I turned back to face the crowd.

"It's kind of like a health club," I said. "We

meet once a week and everyone has to eat a health food lunch under the bleachers in the dark three times before they can become members." I couldn't believe I was saying this.

"What does a ghost have to do with health food?" Eddie asked.

Words jumped out of my mouth again. "Granola, Hominy, Okra, Sprouts, and Tofu," I said. "Those are all health foods. Put the first letter of each word together and they spell GHOST. See? It's easy."

"Hey! That's neat!" said Tim. He smiled down at me and for a second I stared into his twinkling blue eyes. "Can I be a member?" he asked. "I have to stay in training for basketball anyway, so maybe health food is just the thing I need."

"It sounds like a stupid club to me," said Karla. She scrunched her nose up and her glasses hopped. "Why would anyone want to eat that weird-looking stuff anyway?" she asked. "It looks like the kind of stuff they feed to rabbits in pet stores."

"I'd like to join," said Kelly.

"Me, too," Amy echoed.

What good friends I have. I know I can always count on them.

"I'll join," said Eddie. "It sounds just weird enough to be fun. Where do I sign up?"

"Just sign your name on this paper," I said. I pulled a sheet out from my notebook and passed it around. All of a sudden I felt like I was running for president. It was weird. Everyone wanted to join. Even Karla Branhurst signed the sheet. Altogether there were fourteen members, counting me.

"When's the next meeting?" asked Tim.

"Tomorrow at noon under the bleachers," I said. "We'll have to be extra quiet under there since there are so many of us. We don't want to get caught."

"Do we have to bring health food lunches?" asked Eddie.

"That's right," I said. "You can't be a GHOST if you don't eat health food. I'll bring some extra food tomorrow since we have so much of it at home."

It was getting late and Kelly, Amy, and I had a bus to catch. We took off running down the hall and just made it.

That night at home I asked Mom if I could have some extra granola bars in my lunch for the next day. I told her about the new club. She smiled so hard I thought her cheeks were going to crack. She patted me on the head and said, "Billie, darling, I think the club is a wonderful idea! I guess I always knew you'd learn to love health food!"

I didn't tell her the real reason why I started the club. Sometimes it's better to let moms go on thinking exactly what they want to think. And my mom wanted to think that I loved health food. Yuck!

Six

IT took two hands to carry my lunch bag the next day because Mom put so much stuff in it for the other GHOST members. It was mostly the granola bars that made it so heavy. I'd been wondering about getting the recipe from Mom and selling it to the government. I think granola is hard enough to be used for missile silos. The army could build little huts out of it and molasses to hide their weapons in. Nothing could break through those walls.

When lunchtime came, I walked into the gym then made a quick turn under the bleachers. I heard giggling and noise in the very back corner. I walked toward the noise. It took a minute for my eyes to adjust to the darkness. When they did, I saw a group of people sitting on the dusty floor.

"Here she is!" someone said.

"Hi, Billie!"

"Hi, Billie!"

"Hi, President Ghost!"

Giggle, giggle, giggle.

"Sh-sh-sh," I said. "We don't want to get caught." Tim was there. He moved back to make room for me in the circle. I sat down between him and Kelly.

"What did everyone bring?" I asked.

"I brought fruit," said Tim. "Apples." He spilled a bag of apples onto the floor.

"I brought carob cookies," said Amy. "Mom says carob is like fake chocolate. I don't think it tastes as good as real chocolate. But it's *almost* as good, and it's a lot better for you. It doesn't have caffeine in it like real chocolate." Amy passed around her bag of cookies.

It really was kind of neat. All of a sudden we

were all sharing health foods with each other. Arms were reaching and hands were passing vegetables, fruit, and other strange-looking stuff.

It was so dark under the bleachers that we kept bumping our hands and elbows into each other. It seemed like everyone was more relaxed sitting there in the dark, too. People who were usually shy talked more. Even Karla Branhurst seemed pretty nice for a change. She didn't insult me even once.

I reached into my bag to get a granola bar, but instead I grabbed another hand. "Oops!" I said.

"Sorry, Billie." Tim started laughing. "I just couldn't resist another granola bar. Didn't mean to scare you."

I was glad that it was dark because I could feel my face turning the color of strawberry yogurt.

Everyone kept asking me about different kinds of health food. I told them about raisins being good for you because they have iron in them. Bananas are good because they're high in potassium. I told them about eating meatless spaghetti because meat is hard to digest. All of a sudden I felt like a health food expert. It seemed kind of funny because I don't really like the stuff. But in the dark no one could see that I wasn't eating very much of it, so it didn't matter.

The bell rang and Tim said, "Say, Billie. Since your Mom knows a lot about health food, and all the GHOST members need to learn about it, how about if we come over to your house for a health food dinner? OK?"

"Sure," I said. "Fine." I knew that Mom wouldn't mind, but what I didn't know was whether or not I'd mind. I wasn't so sure if I wanted all these people to come to my house and try to eat food that even Bonehead wouldn't eat. But I was glad that Tim wanted to come.

When I asked my mom about it that night, she got real excited. She said, "How simply marvelous! Have your darling little friends come this Saturday!"

I said, "OK." But first I got Mom to promise not to call them "darling little friends" anymore.

When Saturday came, Mom spent most of the afternoon in the kitchen singing and cooking. Sometimes she'd hit a high note and hold it for so long that Bonehead would start to howl. Then Mom would open the kitchen door and throw Bonehead a little piece of rhubarb or monk's beef. Monk's beef isn't beef at all. It's made from—you guessed it—tofu.

Bonehead never ate the scraps, but he'd shut up for a while and crawl into his doghouse. I think it hurt his dog-pride to be given pieces of rhubarb and fake meat.

Then Mom went into her studio and began painting on a large board. She was still singing, but stopped long enough to tell me to take a bath and use her rose salts. The rose salts were a gift from Dad two Christmases ago. They are beautiful pink crystals in a glass bottle, with only enough left for a few more baths, so I knew Mom thought that this was a special evening.

After my bath, I smelled like a rose. I brushed all the tangles out of my hair and put on a denim skirt with a blue pin-striped blouse. Then I set the table.

At six o'clock the front door bell started ringing and I ran to get it. Tim was the first one there. He smiled at me and said, "Hi, Billie. Nice sign!"

Then after Tim came Karla, Amy and Kelly, Eddie, Zippy, Mary Louise and Jill, Terry, and all the rest of them.

"Hi, Billie. Nice sign!" they all said.

I didn't know what sign they were talking about. So I stuck my head out the front door and saw a big painted board in the front yard. It said:

WELCOME ALL LITTLE GHOSTS!!!

A picture of a big green zucchini was painted under the word GHOSTS. Oh, no, I thought. Mom's at it again. Now all the neighbors and my friends will think we're nuts.

"Dinner's almost ready," sang Mom. "But first

let's play a yoga game. It's guaranteed to bring you alpha waves and fill your heart with love."

I was standing in the living room with my friends. "Are you for real?" I asked.

"Why certainly I'm for real, Billie," Mom said. "This is a wonderful little game that helps you to search your heart and teaches you to love your fellow man."

It's at times like these that I wonder if I'm adopted.

"Now everyone choose a partner," said Mom. "Here, Billie. You be partners with this nice young man." She pointed to Tim. "Does everyone have a partner?" Mom asked.

I looked around and everyone was with someone else. My friends all looked like they thought Mom was pretty weird. Probably that's because she is. I could just imagine what Karla Branhurst was going to tell everyone at school.

"Now everyone sit on the floor, facing your partner. Tuck your feet under your bottom. Let your knees touch your partner's knees. Now make your hands into tiger claws. Hold them in front of your shoulders, just barely touching your partner's fingertips."

Tim and I touched knees and fingertips. Everyone else did it, too.

"Now stare into your partner's eyes," said Mom. "Stare, stare, stare. Look into that person's eyes and think about how much you like him or her. Even if you've never talked to this person, stare into your partner's eyes and think about how wonderful this person is."

I couldn't believe that my own mother was embarrassing me like this. But I didn't know what to do, so I stared into Tim's blue eyes. My fingers and knees just barely touched his.

"Stare into the window of your partner's eyes," said Mom. "Let all your goodness flow out to them."

The room was perfectly quiet. I could hear Karla breathing because she has allergies. There was a little smile on Tim's lips. I could see it even though I was looking into his eyes.

You know . . . what's kind of weird is that I really felt like I could see through Tim's eyes. I didn't see his brain or anything like that. But I saw that he was a person just like me with good and bad feelings, hopes and dreams. It was a weird feeling. It was kind of like he was my brother, only better than a brother.

"OK, you've just had your first yoga lesson," said Mom. "You should be feeling some alpha waves by now. Come on. It's time to eat." Everyone got up off the floor, and everyone was smiling.

When we sat down to dinner, I saw some of the kids wrinkle their noses at the food. I guess it looked pretty strange if you weren't used to it. There were bowls of carrot soup, pita bread sandwiches and sprouts, hominy, steamed okra, granola muffins, tofu and cheese soufflé, and peppers stuffed with wheat berries. There was also a platter of monk's beef. For dessert we had rhubarb pudding with bee pollen sprinkled on top.

Mom went out to the kitchen. It was time to eat, but nobody made a move. Finally I started passing bowls and saying stuff like, "M-m-m-m-m, nothing better than a good hunk of monk's beef" and "Mm-m-m-m, smell that okra!" At last everyone put food on his or her plate and started to taste.

"Hey, Billie, this is great!" said Kelly. She held up a fork full of soufflé. "I don't know what you've been crabbing about. This stuff is good!"

"Wow! I've never had carrot soup," said Tim. "This stuff's tasty."

"This sure is better than chicken weiners," said Karla. "That's all my mother ever makes."

I couldn't believe everyone liked Mom's health food so much. I tried to eat some, but the only thing I really liked were the wheat berries.

"Why aren't you eating, Billie?" asked Eddie.

"I'm trying to stay in shape for basketball," I said. "Tryouts are coming up."

"You're not really serious about trying out for the boys' team, are you?" asked Mary Louise.

"Of course I am," I said.

"Then you should probably eat some of the soufflé," said Tim. "Tofu is high in protein. Good for you." He smacked his lips and winked at me.

I took my fork and forced myself to eat the tofu soufflé. It was torture. I'd rather eat an old sock. But I figured I'd give it a try since Tim liked it.

It was really weird because all the kids really liked the health food. They said that the GHOST club was the best club around. They even ate the steamed okra, which if I close my eyes and chew it, reminds me of fish eyeballs.

After dinner we put on some records and danced. My mom came out and danced one dance with us. She grabbed Eddie's hand and he grabbed Jill's hand and she grabbed Tim's hand and he grabbed Amy's hand. I was the last one to grab a hand, so I was last in the line. Then Mom danced all over the room, out to the kitchen, around tables and over chairs. We all followed her in a big, long snakelike line.

It was kind of like Crack-the-Whip. We all laughed and shouted when Mom got down on the floor and crawled under the coffee table. We crawled along right behind her. When the song was over, Mom left the room and we went back to dancing like normal people.

After that first GHOST club meeting and the dinner at my house, some other kids from school wanted to join. Kids started meeting under the bleachers and bringing bags of awful-looking stuff to eat. It seemed like everyone in the whole school started eating health food. Even the kitchen staff started cooking meatless spaghetti when all the kids refused to eat meat.

I couldn't stand it. I used to be able to bum a chicken leg or a cupcake from other people at school. But now everyone's lunch was just as gross as mine. The only difference was that *they* actually liked it.

Seven

IT seemed kind of weird at first to visit Dad's apartment in Columbia City. It was like it couldn't really be his home if Mom and I didn't live there, too. But after a while I got used to visiting. I especially got used to it when I found the huge freezer in Dad's kitchen. It was full of frozen pizzas, egg rolls, cream pies, steaks, ribs, and tons of other stuff. My dad never learned how to cook. I can still remember the fights he and Mom had about it.

After Dad moved to Columbia City, he and I always went grocery shopping as soon as Mom dropped me off. I stuffed the cart with popsicles, dream bars, candied cherries, butterscotch topping, pepperoni, vienna sausages, and chocolate chips.

I cooked a steak dinner for Dad and me one weekend when I was staying there. Dad sat at the kitchen table and we talked. I got Dad to cut the green part off the strawberries for shortcake. We had two cans of whipped cream waiting in the refrigerator.

"How's your love life, Billie?" Dad asked. "Any boyfriends?"

That's what I like about my dad. He never asks me boring stuff like how am I doing in school.

"It stinks, Dad," I said. "Tim Kurtz hasn't even looked at me lately. So I've been working on my basketball. Amy has a hoop."

"Good girl," he said. "Just remember not to shoot in front of your face. Raise the ball over your head. How's that steak doing?"

"It's ready," I said. I cooked it red and juicy just the way we both like it. I could probably eat it raw if Dad would let me.

Dad and I stuffed ourselves with steak, baked potatoes with tons of butter, and French bread with gobs of garlic on it. We were too full after dinner to do anything, so we watched T.V.

When I packed my bag to leave on Sunday morning I asked Dad if I could take some food back with me. He said, "OK," so I went out to the kitchen with my overnight bag.

I ran out of room in my bag, so I had to stuff strawberries left over from the shortcake into my jacket pockets. I knew Dad wouldn't mind because I explained the whole health food diet to him. I think he understood because Mom used to put eucalyptus leaves in his sock drawer. She read in a magazine that it helped your feet to breathe. I don't know about Dad, but my feet never seem to have any problem even in hay fever season.

After I got home I hid the food in my dresser drawer. It was like having a McDonald's right by my bed. Whenever I was hungry at night I just reached over and grabbed a hot dog. They weren't too bad raw. But the strawberries didn't look so great the next day because I left them in my jacket pockets. They were kind of brown and mushy, so I ate them real fast.

Whenever I would get back from Dad's, Mom would say, "Billie, what's happened to your appetite? You eat like a bird."

That made me think of fried chicken. I tried to eat a bowl of Chinese sweet-and-sour soup that Mom passed me at dinner. It had tofu, vinegar, peppers, and honey in it. Talk about gross! Outside, I could hear Bonehead barking his head off in the backyard.

"What's wrong with that silly mutt?" asked Mom. "Billie, would you please go see?"

I just nodded because I had a mouthful of soup. I hurried to the back door and spit it out behind the dragon bush. Bonehead ran up and jumped on me like he always does. But he kept barking and wouldn't stop.

"What's wrong, boy?" I asked.

Sometimes I wish dogs could talk. Usually I

can tell what Bonehead wants, but tonight I couldn't. He finally stopped when I gave him some dog biscuits. I should've known it was food he wanted. I ate half of a dog biscuit and it wasn't too bad, so I ate the other half.

"Billie Joan? Where's your laundry?" called Mom. "Would you gather it together? I'm doing a load right now."

I ran in the house and upstairs to get my stuff. I pulled my jacket out from under my bed and . . . oh, no! It was the jacket that I stuffed the strawberries into. The pockets were kind of pink and moldy. I reached under the bed and pulled out a pair of jeans. Little bits of swiss cheese were stuck in the fuzz in the pockets. I pulled more clothes out. Everything with pockets had food stuck in them. I didn't know what to do. This whole health food thing was beginning to drive me nuts! It's ridiculous when an eleven-year-old girl has to hide food in her pockets, eat dog biscuits, and ask herself over to friends' homes for dinner. I wondered if this was what it was like in Russia.

I stuffed the clothes with moldy pockets into my dresser drawer where I kept the snack food from Dad's. That seemed like a good hiding place. Then I got my socks, underwear and shirts, and took them to Mom.

Right then the phone rang. It was Mrs. Perkins from down the road. She said, "Could you please shut up your darn dog? I can hardly sleep for all the racket."

"Yes, ma'am," I said. "Good-bye."

"Mom! Bonehead woke Mrs. Perkins up!" I yelled. I gave Bonehead some more dog biscuits and he shut up.

The next day when I got home from school there was a van parked in front of the house. A man in a uniform stood on the front porch talking to Mom. When I got closer I saw that his badge said "Barnstown Municipal Volunteer Dog Warden 3."

"I'm sorry, Mrs. Casey," he was saying "I'm afraid we have to take him in. We've had four calls from people complaining."

Suddenly I heard a bark I'd know anywhere and it was coming from the dog warden's van. It was Bonehead! He was locked up in there. His big paws scratched at the window while he barked his head off.

"What's going on, Mom?" I asked. I was feeling pretty nervous. The dog warden didn't look very happy. That's always a bad sign.

"I'm sorry, honey," Mom said, putting her hand on my shoulder. "I'm afraid Bonehead won't stop barking. I just can't seem to do anything with him. I don't know what's come over him."

"Are you taking him to the pound?" I asked the man in the uniform.

He nodded. He didn't look like he liked his job much.

"Are you going to kill him?" I asked.

"I'm afraid we'll have to put him to sleep, Miss," the dog warden said.

"Mom! Are you going to let him do that?"

I cried. "Are you going to let him take Bonehead away?"

I could tell my mom didn't know what to do. I was about ready to scream! My eyes burned with tears.

"I really hate to do this, ma'am," the dog warden said. "I'm just following orders. I've got to take your dog. Don't worry. It won't hurt when we put him to sleep. We just give him a shot. He won't feel a thing."

"Please give us three days," Mom said. "If we can't get him to stop barking in three days you can have him."

The dog warden scratched his chin like he was trying to make up his mind.

"Three days, then you can take him away," Mom said. "I promise."

"OK, ma'am," the dog warden said. "You got a deal. But remember, I'll be back in three days. Then I'll have to take him or I'll lose my job. Now, try to keep that durn mutt quiet."

He walked back to the van and opened the

rear door. Bonehead jumped out, ran back, and almost knocked me and Mom down. The dog warden drove off.

We put Bonehead in the backyard and he was quiet for a while. But as soon as it got dark he started barking and howling. Mom and I took turns going out to pet him and make him keep quiet. We were up most of the night and I was tired in school the next day.

On the second night Bonehead started barking again. Two people called us to say he was waking them up. I took my blanket downstairs and slept on the kitchen floor so I could run outside quickly and make him quit yipping and yapping.

When he wasn't barking I lay on the kitchen floor and thought about all the great times Bonehead and I had had together. He was so cute when he first jumped out of that white box. He licked my face whenever I cried. He always put his paw in my lap when he wanted to be loved. When I scratched his head in just the right way he'd shake his back leg. It was like he had a string attached from his ear to his hind foot.

And now they were going to take him away from me. They were going to "put him to sleep." That's just a nice way of saying you're going to kill somebody. How could they do that? Kill Bonehead? How could I let them? What could I do?

Just then Bonehead started to bark again. I rushed outside to pet his head and I held his paw. I sat on the porch with him and watched the stars. There was a cloud passing over the moon. Bonehead whacked me on the ear with his tail.

Good old dog. Boy, did I love him! I'd never let the dog warden take him! NEVER, N-E-V-E-R!!!

The next day when I got home from school Mom told me that the dog warden called and he was bringing the van to get Bonehead tomorrow. The warden said that since the dog was still barking we only had one night left to make him keep quiet. Mom looked like she'd been crying. Her lipstick was smeared and her nose was pink.

That night when Bonehead started barking Mom hung her head and said, "Well, I guess this is Bonehead's last night with us."

"No, Mom," I yelled. "It can't be!"

"Well, what else can we do?" she asked.

"Let's bring him in the house," I said. Suddenly it seemed like a great idea. "He won't bark if he's in here," I said.

"I guess we can try it," said Mom doubtfully.

I ran and brought Bonehead inside. But it seemed like he started barking even more. He started running in circles and snarling like a wild tiger.

Mom and I chased him around the house while he knocked lamps over and galloped over chairs. It was like Bonehead suddenly went crazy.

We followed him from room to room then upstairs as he raced into my bedroom and jumped onto my bed.

"Bonehead! Stop that!" Mom yelled.

Bonehead started clawing and scratching at my dresser.

Awr-ooo-ooo, he howled. *Awr-ooo-ooo.*

Mom ran over to the dresser and grabbed Bonehead by the collar. Then she opened the drawer where he'd been scratching.

"Eeee-e-e-e!" Mother yelled. "Belinda Joan Casey! What is this? What have you done?"

I ran to the drawer and looked in. There was a whole family of baby mice living in my jeans pocket. Mice must love swiss cheese. There were cracker crumbs in there, too. It must've been like living in a grocery store to them. I'd forgotten all about the clothes with food stuffed in the pockets. Boy, was I in trouble.

My mother called an exterminator the next day. Exterminators are people who come over to your house and get rid of pests like mice and bugs. I wonder if I could get one to come to my school and get rid of Karla Branhurst.

Mom called the dog warden. She explained

the whole thing to him about how Bonehead was only barking because he knew there were mice in the house. He only barked at night because that's when mice come out to eat. She explained that Bonehead knew the mice were there, but that we didn't. The dog warden said we could keep Bonehead.

Bonehead quit barking when we got rid of the mice. We got rid of the dog warden when Bonehead quit barking.

Now that Bonehead's safe it seems kind of funny when I think about it. I mean, even the mice were going crazy in my house. They were all just scrambling around trying to find something good to eat. The mice must hate mung beans, dried carrots, and all that other gross health food stuff just as much as I do. I mean, I wouldn't mind living in someone's jeans pocket if it had chocolate bars and cheeseburgers in it.

Eight

BY late Fall I was up to Plan 47. This plan was to spend every weekend at my dad's. I decided I couldn't stand it at home anymore when Mom made me eat a bowl of cold beet soup. She tried to fool me into liking it by telling me that the Russians eat beet soup every day. Right before the beet soup, she made me wear a copper bracelet so I wouldn't get arthritis. She read in a magazine about how copper is good for you.

Before that she took my foam rubber pillow away and gave me one stuffed with Irish duck feathers. She said I'd sleep better with it. But since I sleep okay anyway, it didn't make much difference. Besides, sometimes at school I'd find little duck feathers stuck in my hair. Karla Branhurst started asking me if I was working in a chicken factory.

I spent the whole week at school thinking of great food to get when I got to Dad's. I planned to spend every weekend for the rest of my life at his apartment, eating and drinking junk food. Finally the weekend came and Mom dropped me off in Columbia City.

"Let's go grocery shopping, Dad," I said as soon as Mom left. But Dad had other plans

"I've fixed dinner for us tonight," Dad said. "We don't need to go shopping."

I couldn't believe it! Dad was cooking dinner. It made me feel really special, because he never used to cook at home.

"What are we having, Dad?" I asked. "Hot fudge sundaes?"

Dad shook his head. "Not tonight, Billie," he said. "How about pork chops and brussels sprouts?"

"Are you kidding, Dad?" I ran to the freezer

and looked in. There wasn't even one frozen cream pie in there . . . just boxes of peas and one chicken pot pie.

"What's the joke, Dad?" I asked. This was beginning to look serious.

"Billie, let's have a little talk," Dad said.

I might be only eleven years old, but one thing I've figured out is that if your dad says he wants to have a "little" talk, he really means a "big" talk.

"Billie," Dad said, "let me know if I'm wrong, but lately it seems like you're just coming here to eat. Does it seem that way to you?"

I couldn't think of anything to say, because he was right. I was coming there just to eat. It's not the sort of thing you like to admit to your dad.

"Your mom and I have been talking," Dad said. "We've decided that it might be better if you don't come to visit me quite so often. Your mother feels—and I agree with her—that you need to spend more time at home. I'm sorry, hon. That's just the way it is."

I couldn't help it. I started to cry. It was just too much! My own dad was telling me he didn't want to see me anymore!

"But, Dad," I sobbed, "you don't understand. She makes me eat sprouts on everything. I can't have any sugar. Bonehead's food tastes better than mine. She tries to fool me by putting tofu in milk shakes. Even the mice can't stand it!" I sounded a little like Bonehead howling, but I couldn't help it. Some girls look cute when they cry, but not me.

"Billie!" Dad came over and put his arms around me. That's what I like about my dad. He's the kind of guy who squeezes you when you feel like no one in the whole world understands you.

"Is it really that bad, Billie?" asked Dad.

I wiped my nose on my sleeve. "I'm going nuts," I said. "I want to live with you. Can I divorce Mom? YOU did it! Why can't I? Can I divorce Mom like YOU did? Can I?"

Suddenly I felt like I was a terrible kid, maybe even the worst kid in Ohio. My Dad just sat there and looked kind of sad. He doesn't like to talk about the divorce. Whenever I bring it up, his eyes start to droop like he's getting sleepy.

"I'm sorry, Dad," I said.

"It's OK, Billie," Dad said. "I understand."

I don't know if he really did understand or not, but I think he was at least trying.

"Maybe, Billie," Dad said, "you could try a little harder with your mother. This is a rough time for her. It's rough for all of us. But you could help by trying to understand your mother a little more."

See what I mean? Whenever they tell you there's a "little" talk coming you can bet it's going to be a whopper of a talk.

That night at Dad's I did a lot of thinking. I decided that I really do love my mom, even if she is weird. It's just that sometimes I forget I love her. Sometimes I forget I love my dad, too. But I never forget that I love Bonehead. I wonder why that is. Maybe it's because dogs don't make you eat tofu and mung beans.

But I decided I'd try harder. I'd learn to eat that goat food and like it. I'd make Dad proud of me. Tomorrow when I got home I'd ask Mom if we had any pumpkin seeds to nibble on, or maybe some dried apricots.

The next morning Dad and I went to a fast-food place for breakfast. I only got one cinnamon roll instead of two, like I usually get. I didn't want Dad to think I love food more than I love him.

After that Mom picked me up at Dad's. But first she came in for a cup of herbal tea. They talked about boring stuff like needing the oil changed in the car and how the sleeves on my fall coat are too short.

It seems weird to see my mom and dad together when I know they're not married anymore. But I'm getting used to it. Sometimes I wish Mom would get married again, because then I'd have *two* dads. But my mom's so weird that probably she couldn't get anyone to marry her. Anyway, I don't think she wants to get married again. Most moms would, but not mine.

Nine

PLAN 48 was the hardest plan of all. This was the plan where I was going to try to like everything that Mom cooked, even if it had fish eyeballs in it.

I'd been at Amy's shooting baskets all day. When I got home the house looked different. It was clean for a change. Usually we have dust balls that roll with you when you walk down the hall. To tell you the truth, I kind of like them. They're like little hedgehogs.

"Hey, Mom!" I yelled. "What's happened to the house?" Even the front window was clean where I leave nose marks. I like to stand close to it when I watch leaves fall outside.

"We're having company for dinner," Mom said. "Get cleaned up and brush your hair, please."

Mom seemed nervous. All her alpha waves must have escaped.

"Who's coming?" I asked.

Right then the door bell rang. I ran to see who it was. I opened the door and there was a strange man standing there. He held a hat in one hand and a book in the other. "How do you do?" he asked. "May I come in?"

"Of course, Clement," Mom said, rushing up.

Clement? What a weird name. I'd never heard of a man called Clement before. Who was this guy? What did he want with my mom?

"I brought you a book, Margaret," he said. "It's all about ranching."

"Are you a cowboy?" I asked.

"Belinda! Of course he's not a cowboy. Mr. O'Hanlon is a farmer. He owns that big farm right outside of Barnstown. You know, the one by Moon Pond?"

"The one with all the cows?" I asked.

"That's the one," Mr. O'Hanlon said.

So Mom had a date. I couldn't believe it. . . . My mom with a date! So that's why the house was so clean. Bonehead didn't even smell as bad as he usually did. I should've known right then something was up.

Mr. O'Hanlon sat down while Mom went out to the kitchen. "How's school going, Billie?" he asked.

"Fine," I said. My dad would never ask a question like that. I made my stomachache face at Mr. O'Hanlon and hoped he wouldn't ask me any more dumb questions.

"Dinner's ready!" Mom called.

Mr. O'Hanlon and I went to the dining room. The table was covered with a white cloth, and a bowl of roses sat in the middle. The glasses were shining and the napkins were made out of cloth. Everything was different. I was glad to see at least Mom used the old dishes with chips in them. But then, they're the only dishes we have. I like those old chips. They're like little friends.

Mom lifted the cover off of the platter and I almost screamed, but I didn't. Instead, I pinched myself under the table to make sure I wasn't dreaming. There on the platter was a whole stack of roast beef slices with steam rising off them. It was cooked with the middle still pink, just the way I like it. In a bowl was thick brown gravy, and in a basket were crumbling white rolls with butter oozing out the sides. I almost fainted when I saw jello with bananas and blackberries in it and whipped cream on top.

"Where's the tofu, Mom?" I asked. "Where's the seaweed?"

"Oh, Billie," Mom said. She wrinkled her forehead at me. "I read a very interesting article in a magazine the other day. It said that red meat is good for your blood and it puts shine in your hair." Then Mom winked at me. "Here, honey," she said, "have some strawberry jam on your roll."

I almost fainted again. "No, thanks," I said. "I'd rather have some bean sprouts."

I don't know what made me say that. I think

I just finally got tired of everyone telling me what to do. Eat this, Billie. Drink this, Billie. Don't put strawberries in your pockets, Billie. Don't cross your eyes, Billie, or they'll get stuck. I just couldn't take it anymore.

Mom's lips began to disappear. "Billie," she said, "Mr. O'Hanlon was nice enough to give us this beef from his farm. I hope you won't embarrass me by being rude."

If you ask me, I think it was Mom who was being rude. I don't think parents should yell at their kids in front of other people. It's embarrassing. It makes me feel like Bonehead.

"That's all right, Margaret," Mr. O'Hanlon said. "My feelings won't be hurt. I've got tougher skin than that. Let Billie eat what she wants to eat."

I looked more closely at Mr. O'Hanlon. His eyes were brown and they kind of twinkled when he smiled. He looked like the kind of guy who would understand. So I explained to him, "You see, I'm president of the GHOST club. It's a health food club at school."

"Do you like health food?" asked Mr. O' Hanlon.

"Some of it is okay," I said. "I like wheat berries and I like fruit. But some of it is just plain gross. And besides, I miss eating meat and sugar."

"You should eat what you want to eat," said Mr. O'Hanlon. "I'm sure you're a sensible girl."

"But what about the club?" I asked. "I'm the president and I'd probably get thrown out if I got caught eating meat or junk food. We have to eat health food. That's why we named ourselves the GHOST club. The letters stand for vegetables."

Mr. O'Hanlon took a bite of his buttered biscuit. It sure did look good.

"Change the name," he said between bites.

It's funny. I never even thought of changing the club's name. I tried to think of a new name, but the only thing I could think of was the SCMHPAMS club. That stood for "Snickers, Candy, Meat, Honey, Pizzas, And More Snickers." But that was too long to remember. Besides that, I didn't know how to pronounce it. So I tried to think of a shorter name. It had to be something short, simple, and tasty. I looked at the table and stared at the platter of beef with potatoes around it.

That's it!" I said. "Meat and Potatoes. We'll be the MAP club. It's easy to remember, and meat's high in protein and potatoes are a vegetable. We can still be a health food club and eat meat!"

"That's a delightful name!" cried Mom. "The MAP Club. That's sweet."

"There's only one problem," I said. I looked at Mom, who had a little smear of strawberry jam on her mouth. "Am I going to have to change the name of this club every time you go on a new diet?" I asked.

"Why, Billie Casey! Whatever makes you say such a thing?" asked Mom.

"Because you make me sleep on duck feathers, wear copper bracelets, sleep in sleeping bags, and eat whatever you eat. Don't you think I'm old enough to decide some things for myself?" I asked.

Mom thought about it for a minute. At first I was afraid she might start humming and doing her yoga exercises right in front of Mr. O'Hanlon.

But instead she said, "Billie, my sweet, you're absolutely right! You've been trying to grow up, and I've been trying to hold you back. I guess I've been afraid of losing my little girl. But you know what? I'll love the young woman just as much! I'm sorry, honey. Moms make mistakes sometimes."

Wow! I thought I might be dreaming so I pinched myself again. That's what I like about my mom. She's not embarrassed to admit it when she's wrong. Neither am I.

I said, "I guess food's not that important anyway. When you stop and think about it, all the food ends up in your stomach. Once it's there you can't tell a chocolate bar from a tofu burger."

Mom and Mr. O'Hanlon laughed at that. You should have seen them sitting there, smiling at each other and at me. I wondered if Mom liked Mr. O'Hanlon half as much as I liked Tim Kurtz. I think she did because she asked him if he wanted more whipped cream on his jello. I wondered if Mr. O'Hanlon knew that Mom cuts bushes into duck and dragon shapes for a living.

"Mom, may I be excused to go over to Amy's to practice basketball?" I asked.

"Certainly," said Mom. "Give your scraps to Bonehead first."

"Are you a basketball player?" asked Mr. O'Hanlon.

"I will be," I said. "Tryouts for next year's team are next week. I'm going to be the first girl in Barnstown to make it on the team!"

Mr. O'Hanlon looked at me. He looked like Dad used to when he watched me swim six laps without stopping in the public pool.

"You know, Billie," Mr. O'Hanlon said, "you'd be a match for anyone! I'll bet you one double fudge banana split that you'll make it!"

Mom blew me a big kiss from across the table. "I think you can do it, too, sugar," she said.

I heard Bonehead barking in the backyard. I think he was saying he thought I could do it, too, and do you know what? All three of them were right! When tryouts came up I out jumped and out hustled everyone I could. I knew I'd have to try harder since I'm shorter than most of the guys. But I made it. I'm the very first girl to become a member of the boys' basketball team in Barnstown. Maybe it was eating all that health food that kept me in shape. I don't know. But one thing I do know is that I've started eating some health food regularly. It doesn't seem so awful now that I'm eating it on my own and no one's forcing me.

I'm still president of the MAP club. It keeps getting bigger and bigger. You'll never guess who is vice-president. It's Tim Kurtz! I still like to stare into his blue eyes. But it's kind of hard to see them when we're in the dark under the bleachers with the rest of the club. But there's one thing I know for sure.

Whenever I'm around him I start feeling alpha waves. At least that's what I think they are. I feel happy and kind of dreamy. I guess I have my mom to thank for that. She might be a little on the strange side with all of her weird yoga exercises. But I know that when I hear that humming and I see Mom's eyes closed, she's filling her heart with love and happiness. I guess that's a neat kind of mom to have.

About the Author

Janet Adele Bloss lives in Ohio with her husband, Ron, and two children, Matthew and Suzanne. When Janet isn't writing, she likes to play with her kids—climb trees, stomp in mud puddles, and go on flashlight hikes at night.

Janet says, "When people read my books, they're getting a peek into my daydreams. It's fun to share my dreams. I love writing for kids because they have such great imaginations."

Janet visits schools and talks to students about writing. She sometimes gets ideas for her stories from the kids she talks with. "If I'm going to write for kids, I need to hear what they have to say. Kids might be little, but their ideas are big."